2052

The Day the Sun Danced

by Edith Thacher Hurd

Pictures by Clement Hurd

Harper & Row, Publishers • *New York*

ESEA — TITLE II

To Ursula

THE DAY THE SUN DANCED

Text copyright © 1965 by Edith Thacher Hurd

Pictures copyright © 1965 by Clement Hurd

Library of Congress Catalog Card Number: 64-16641

The brook was quiet.
It did not move.
It was frozen quiet and still.
It was winter.

The brown earth was quiet.
Nothing moved in the brown earth.
It was frozen quiet and still.
It was winter.

Not even a small bug moved.
Not even an earthworm turned
in the cold ground.
Even the frogs seemed frozen.
They lay so quiet and still.

The trees had no leaves.
The wind, the rain, and the snow,
the wild storms of winter,
had torn all of the leaves
off the trees.

There were no birds anywhere
to sing in the dark winter.
Only an old black crow cawed, coldly.

Winter was in the sky, dark and gray.
Winter was deep in the brown earth.

The animals—the bear,
the fox, and the deer—
slept in dark holes,
rock caves,
and deep in the woods.

The winter was cold, cold,
cold under the fur and into the bones
of the bear, the fox, and the deer.
Only the rabbit stirred.
He hopped about a little
because he was restless.
Something was going to happen.

The rabbit went to the deer.
"Come out of the woods," he said.
"Come to the high hill with me.
Come when there is no light
but most of the night is gone."
But the deer would not come.
The rabbit went to the fox.
"Come out of your den," he said.

"Come out of that cold dark hole.
Come to the top of the hill with me.
Something is going to happen."
But the fox would not come.
The rabbit said to the bear:
"Come out of your cave in the rocks.
Come to the high hill with me.
Something is going to happen."
But the bear would not come.

"The world is too dark and too cold,"
said the bear, the fox, and the deer.
"And besides, what could a foolish rabbit know
that we do not?"
"I know that something is going to happen,"
said the rabbit,
"because I have not slept all winter
in a dark hole, or a cave.
I have not stayed deep in the woods.
I have visited many places in the snow.
I know that something is going to happen.
The world is going to change."

At last the bear, the fox, and the deer
became restless too,
and they went to the top of the hill with the rabbit.
They went in the dark time,
just before the earliest part of the day,
just before daylight.

The rabbit, the bear, the fox, and the deer
waited on the top of the high hill.
They waited in the darkness.
And it was cold,
cold, cold,
cold under the fur and into the bones
of the bear, the fox, and the deer.
They wanted to go home, but the rabbit said:
"No, wait."
And they waited.

Suddenly it happened.
The SUN!
The sun was there in the darkness.
The glorious gold-bright sun
sprang up from behind the hill.

The sun was green.
It was purple.
It was red.
The sun was a glorious pinwheel.
Green, purple, and red,
blood-red.
Then it was white, gold-white.

The sun danced.
The golden white sun rose out of the darkness
and danced in the black winter sky.

The rabbit felt the warm sun
on his long cold ears.
The bear felt the sun creep
through his heavy brown fur.
The fox stretched in the new warmness.

The deer ran,
leaping and jumping
down the hill.

The sun rose higher.
It touched the top of a tall pine tree
where the old crow
waited to warm himself in the sun.

The rabbit was right.
Something had happened.
And the world began to change,
for every day after that the sun rose up
over the hill and warmed the world.
The small brook stirred deep under its
ice covering.
The brook began to move again as
the sun turned the ice into water.
The frogs came out of the cold hard mud
and sang again.

The sun warmed the earth where the snow
had lain white and cold for so long.
Small bugs moved, and worms turned in the earth.
Roots deep in the ground began to move again.
Green things began to grow everywhere.

The bear, the fox, and the deer did not go
back into the cave in the rock,
into the dark hole,
or deep in the woods
where they had spent the winter.
The animals were too thin and hungry.
They hunted.
And they ate the new growing things.
The sun warmed the animals.
And they lay down to rest.

The sun warmed the green growing things
and they were flowers:
mayflowers,
trilliums,
white and golden violets.
Flowers were everywhere:
in the woods,
beside the small brook,
and in the open meadow
where a warm wind blew.
The birds came back to build their nests again.

It was not long before
there were blue eggs
warmed by the sun
in the robin's nest.

The sun warmed a cluster of tiny black eggs.
The frog had left them in a quiet pool by the brook.
The eggs moved and there were tadpoles everywhere.

The days passed,
one after another.
The sun found the cave in the rocks
and warmed the old mother bear
and her newborn cubs.

The sun warmed the deer
with her fawn in the woods.

In the den of the fox,
small foxes fought one another
in the warm sunlight.

The darkness was gone.
The coldness was gone.
The winter was gone.
It was spring!
And everywhere the sun danced!

Date Due

Dec. 13			
NOV 2 6 1960			
JAN 20			
JAN 5			
MAR 2 1971			
APR 1 1 1984			
APR 2 8 1983			
MAR 5			
FEB 1			
FEB 8 1			
FEB 2 8			